This Walker book belongs to:

_____

_____

_____

For Amelia, Audrey and

Brooklyn the Chicken

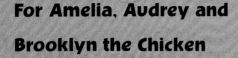

First published 1998 by Walker Books Ltd
87 Vauxhall Walk, London SE11 5HJ

This edition published 2017

10 9 8 7 6 5 4 3 2 1

© 1998 Sue Heap

The right of Sue Heap to be identified as author/illustrator of this work has been
asserted by her in accordance with the Copyright, Designs and Patents Act 1988

This book has been typeset in Opti Bevis Bold

Printed in China

British Library Cataloguing in Publication Data:
a catalogue record for this book is available from the British Library.

ISBN: 978-1-4063-8018-7

www.walker.co.uk

Cowboy Baby

Sue Heap

WALKER BOOKS

AND SUBSIDIARIES

LONDON · BOSTON · SYDNEY · AUCKLAND

It was getting late and Sheriff Pa said, "Cowboy Baby, time for bed."

But Cowboy Baby wouldn't go to bed, not without Texas Ted and Denver Dog and Hank the Horse.

"Off you go and find them," said Sheriff Pa. "Bring them safely home."

Cowboy Baby put on his
hat and his boots, and
he set off on the trail of
Texas Ted, Denver Dog
and Hank the Horse.

He went down the
dusty path and through
the barnyard gate.
Over by the hen-house
he found . . .

Texas Ted.

"Howdy, Texas Ted," said Cowboy Baby.

Cowboy Baby and Texas Ted
crossed the rickety bridge.
Down by the old wagon
wheel they found . . .

Denver Dog.

"Howdy, Denver Dog," said Cowboy Baby.

Cowboy Baby, Texas Ted and
Denver Dog crawled through
the long grass and out into
the big, wide desert.

There by the little
rock they found . . .

Hank the Horse.

"Howdy, Hank the Horse," said Cowboy Baby.

"I'VE FOUND THEM,"
Cowboy Baby shouted to Sheriff Pa.

"That's dandy," Sheriff Pa called back.
"Bring them home now,
safe and sound."

Cowboy Baby and his gang
sat down on the little rock.
None of them wanted
to go home.

"Let's hide!" said
Cowboy Baby.

"Hey, Sheriff Pa," he shouted,
"I bet you can't find us,
        NO SIRREE!"

Sheriff Pa came to the big,
wide desert.
"Shh!" said Cowboy Baby
to his gang.

He looked . . .   and he looked . . .

and he looked.

But he couldn't find
Cowboy Baby.
No sirree!
"You got me beat,
Cowboy Baby,"
called Sheriff Pa.

"But if you come
out, there'll be
a big surprise,
just for you!"

Out jumped Cowboy Baby.
"Howdy, Sheriff Pa!"

The sheriff
threw his lasso.
It twisted and
turned in the
starlit sky,
and it caught . . .

a twinkling
star.

"Look!" said Sheriff Pa,
and he gave the
star to Cowboy Baby.
"Now you're my
deputy," he said.

Then Cowboy Baby picked up Texas Ted

and Denver Dog

and Hank the Horse,

and Sheriff Pa picked
up Cowboy Baby.
And all together they
went home . . .

to bed.

"Nighty night,
Cowboy Baby,"
said Sheriff Pa.

But Cowboy Baby
was already fast
asleep.

YES SIRREE!